Clarity and the Wisdom Tree

Written by Debra Quercetti

Illustrated by Carla Joseph

Copyright © 2022 Debra Quercetti

Written by Debra Quercetti
Illustrated by Carla Joseph

Published by Miriam Laundry Publishing Company
miriamlaundry.com

Also available in French and Spanish

HC ISBN 978-1-998816-09-5
PB ISBN 978-1-998816-07-1
e-Book ISBN 978-1-998816-08-8

FIRST EDITION

 debraquercetti.com    @DebraQuercettiAuthor   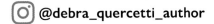 @debra_quercetti_author

To children everywhere who sparkle
with an awesome zest for life,

May they listen to their own
truths, believe in themselves and
grow into exactly the people
they want to be.

One day, Clarity was walking in the forest near her home with her parents, her brother Paul, and her dog, Luna.

The brown walking paths were wide and smooth, made from soft mulch. Clarity took a deep breath and liked how fresh the forest smelled.

She looked at the trees — so many different trees in all shades of green — and she wondered what it was like to stand still all day and all night.

Did they ever get tired?
Did they ever get lonely?

Clarity spotted an old, decaying tree standing in the middle of a circle of very healthy, giant fir trees.

"What kind of tree is that?"

Her brother answered, "It's just an old, dead tree!"

But Clarity's father said, "It's a grandparent tree, likely 1,000 years old, and as it dies, it gives up its nutrients to support all the trees around it."

7

8

"This tree is also known as a spirit tree," her mother added. "It is full of wisdom. If you sit very still under it and ask a question, the tree will hear you. If you listen carefully, you will feel the tree's answer."

Was this true? Clarity wondered.
Will the tree talk to me?

She heard leaves rustling in the wind. *Are the trees speaking?* Clarity smiled at her dog, Luna, curled up asleep in the roots of the grandfather tree.

Clarity thought about the spirit tree for the rest of the day.

That night, she dreamt that she was sitting quietly under the tree, meditating and listening to its words of wisdom.

10

The next day at school, there was a new girl in Clarity's class. Holly had curly brown hair and bright green eyes. She got a perfect mark on her spelling test and bonus points for spelling a very hard word.

One of Clarity's friends called her smarty pants.

13

At lunchtime, Clarity said,
"Let's ask Holly to sit with us."
One friend rolled her eyes.

Another girl said, "I'm not
eating with the teacher's pet."

In her heart, Clarity knew that it must be hard for Holly being new at school, and she wanted to find a way to make her feel welcome. *Maybe I can ask the spirit tree for an answer.*

The next day was Saturday. Clarity hopped on her bike, pigtails flying in the wind as she pedaled to the forest.

When she arrived at the circle of trees, Clarity sat down and leaned into the wisdom tree's trunk. She touched its bark, closed her eyes and listened to the birds.

Breathing slowly, she imagined herself inside the tree. She smelled the wood and felt the circular walls embrace her.

She could hear the tree humming a beautiful lullaby.

Soon, Clarity heard the tree murmuring to her.

I am a tree. Tall and sturdy as you can see. The sunlight helps me grow, and my leaves reach high up to the sky. The rain tickles my roots as they grow deep underground, seeking water and food to feed myself and my family.

21

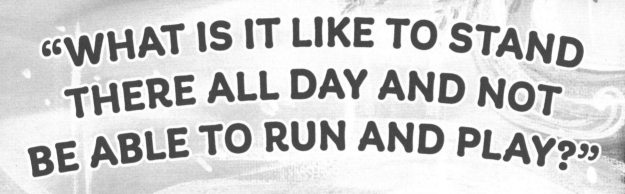

"WHAT IS IT LIKE TO STAND THERE ALL DAY AND NOT BE ABLE TO RUN AND PLAY?"

It's true I can't run or play. But my branches bend with the wind, and sometimes they touch my brothers' and sisters' arms.

In the winter it is hard work to hold all the snow, and when it gets too heavy, I let it go. That's when you'd better not be below!

23

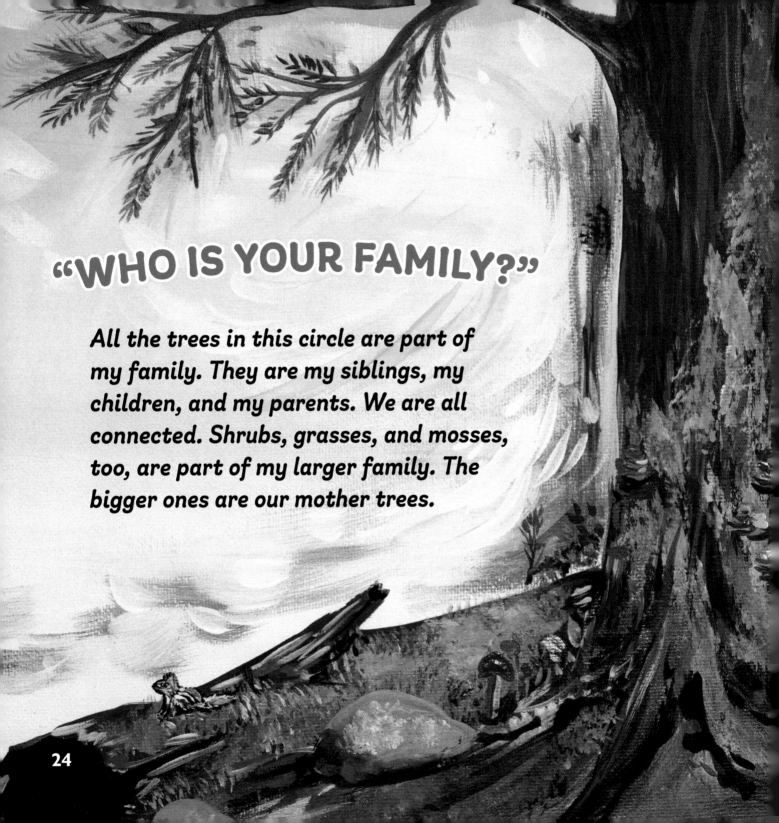

"WHO IS YOUR FAMILY?"

All the trees in this circle are part of my family. They are my siblings, my children, and my parents. We are all connected. Shrubs, grasses, and mosses, too, are part of my larger family. The bigger ones are our mother trees.

Like me, they make sure that the younger ones are fed, and the older ones and sick ones are cared for. We feed them through our roots.

"ARE YOU EVER LONELY?"

Never! Besides having my plant family, all the forest creatures live happily among us. Squirrels, raccoons, and chipmunks play in my branches, and birds nest here, too. Deer and eagles are my friends. They bring me news from faraway places. And during the day, I enjoy the people walking, running, or biking by. My favorite times are when people like your dad introduce you to me!

"DO YOU GET SCARED AT NIGHT?"

Why would I? On a clear night, I gaze upon thousands of stars that twinkle, and the moon winks back at me. On a cloudy night, the clouds comfort me like a warm blanket.

28

Clarity thought about Holly.
She felt the tree embrace
her more snugly.

Clarity, listen carefully.

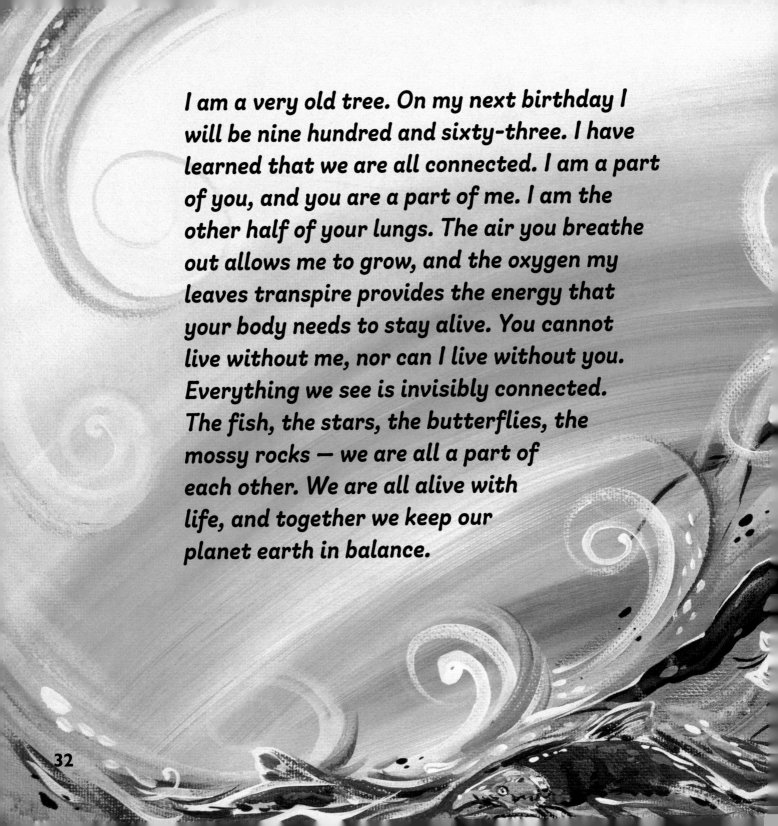

I am a very old tree. On my next birthday I will be nine hundred and sixty-three. I have learned that we are all connected. I am a part of you, and you are a part of me. I am the other half of your lungs. The air you breathe out allows me to grow, and the oxygen my leaves transpire provides the energy that your body needs to stay alive. You cannot live without me, nor can I live without you. Everything we see is invisibly connected. The fish, the stars, the butterflies, the mossy rocks — we are all a part of each other. We are all alive with life, and together we keep our planet earth in balance.

Humm... Clarity felt her body relax. She knew that what the spirit tree said was true.

So ... if everything is connected, then I'm connected to Holly and she to me. So ... so ... I should treat Holly the way I'd want to be treated! If I was the new girl, I'd ... I'd want to eat lunch with a friend.

Clarity sensed the tree smiling. She felt herself slowly being released from its embrace.

Deer Foot Path

When she opened her eyes, she saw Holly riding her bike along Deerfoot Path.

Holly stopped beside her and looked up at the spirit tree. "Did you know that trees can talk?" she asked.

Clarity nodded. "And do you know that this is a wisdom tree? Do you know that trees are the other half of our lungs?" Holly smiled, and both girls giggled.

And there and then, under the wisdom tree, Clarity knew she had found a very special friend.

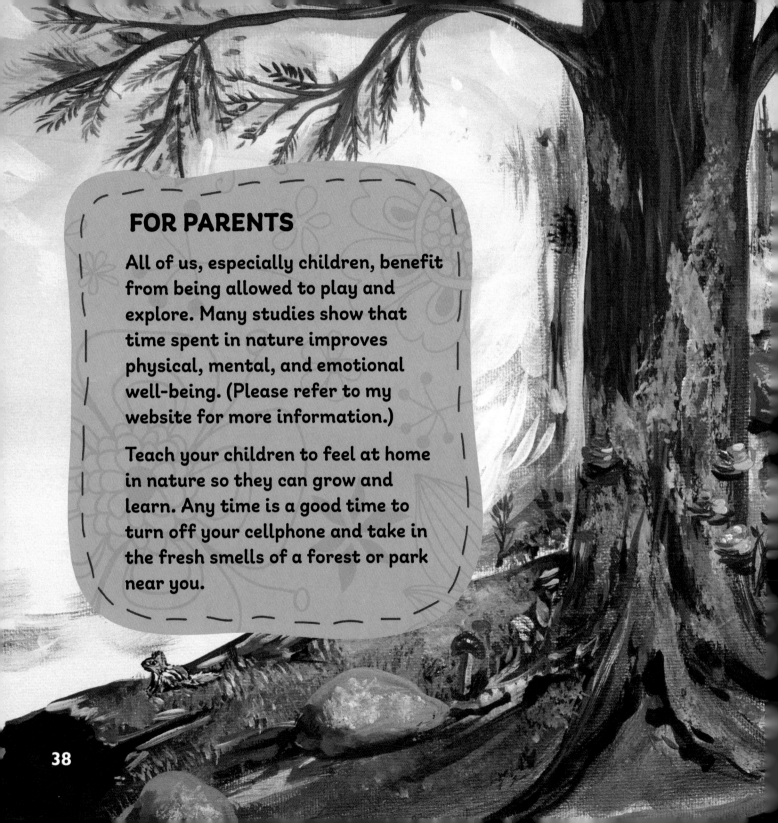

FOR PARENTS

All of us, especially children, benefit from being allowed to play and explore. Many studies show that time spent in nature improves physical, mental, and emotional well-being. (Please refer to my website for more information.)

Teach your children to feel at home in nature so they can grow and learn. Any time is a good time to turn off your cellphone and take in the fresh smells of a forest or park near you.

FOR YOUNGER CHILDREN

With toddlers and pre-schoolers, just start to explore. Keep the walks short, and let the child lead. Listen for birds or frogs; look for mushrooms and bugs. See and feel the mossy rocks and tree barks. Smell everything. Take friends and give names to the trees and plants. Play. Find hiding spots, lay or roll on the ground, get dirty, climb on stumps, and jump in puddles. Go back to familiar areas again and again.

FOR OLDER CHILDREN

Make the walks age appropriate. Look for mushrooms and berries, being careful not to touch or eat anything that you don't know is safe. Determine if you can see traces of woodpeckers or animal droppings. Ask questions. Encourage your children to draw what they see or take rubbings from the bark. Post these around the house. Take a photo of the same picture in each of the seasons, and compare the pictures.

Always remember to take care of nature. If you have a picnic, take your garbage home with you. We would never want to harm the animals that live in the forest or the beautiful nature around us.

ABOUT THE AUTHOR

Debra lives in Vancouver, BC with her dog, Luna. Her daily walks in Pacific Spirit Park provided the inspiration for this book. As an early lover of nature, walking in the woods or along the shores of Vancouver's beaches provided a welcome respite from a busy life. Spending time in nature, especially going into the woods, often provides a mental refresh that Debra feels is an important skill for all people in today's fast-paced society. Debra believes that teaching young souls to sit still, listen and wonder is an important aspect for their developing minds. She has studied as a mystic and believes that the true essence of world religions and basic human kindness principles need to be taught at an early age. This is Debra's first foray into children's literature. She hopes to continue teaching through more stories about *Clarity and the Wisdom Tree*.

ABOUT THE ILLUSTRATOR

Carla Joseph is a Metis Cree artist born in Prince George, BC. Carla received her key to become an artist while in residence at the Prince George Community Arts Council in 2016. She went on to win Art Battle in 2016 and 2018.

Carla has her own unique style which many people look forward to experiencing. She loves the way she makes people feel with her art, and it inspires her to continue with her gift. Carla loves to challenge herself by taking on many different projects that can be seen around her home community and all over Canada.

Carla has illustrated four children's books, over 20 murals, logos and other wonderful projects.

Manufactured by Amazon.ca
Bolton, ON

29863645R00026